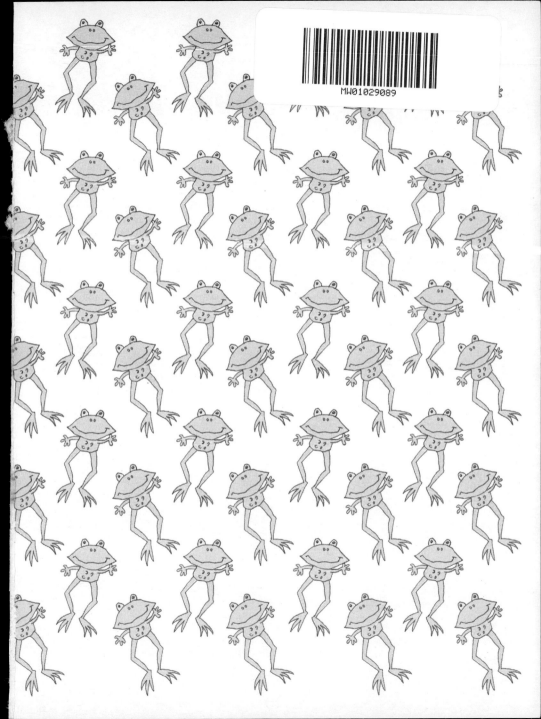

First published in Great Britain 2015
by Jelly Pie an imprint of Egmont UK Ltd
The Yellow Building, 1 Nicholas Road, London W11 4AN

Text and illustration copyright © Angie Morgan 2015
The moral rights of the author–illustrator have been asserted.

ISBN 978 1 4052 7512 5

www.jellypiecentral.co.uk
www.egmont.co.uk

A CIP catalogue record for this title is available from the British Library

Printed and bound in Great Britain by the CPI Group

58653/3

# Sedric
### AND THE
## HAIRY TROLL INVASION

# Angie Morgan

Before you start this book - here is some stuff about my village.

# LITTLE SOGGY-IN-THE-MUD

which is small and very muddy and can be found in the bottom right hand corner of **BRITAIN** where it goes all pointy. I live there with my mum Ethel and my dad Wilfred. There are some ~~a few~~ **HOVELS** (not sure how many) and they are very **LEAKY** and **WET**☆

There is a **PIGSTY** (which is sometimes used by visitors who don't mind the smell.)

a **SCHOOL** (WELL boring)

skool

There is also lots of **MUD**

We eat **LOADS** of turnip

Turnip field where we grow TURNIPS

There are also ~~some~~ a **LOT** of **RATS**

☆ owing to the enormous quantities of **RAIN**.

On the edge of the village is the

## DARK FOREST →

which is full of TROLLS
and GIANT HOBGOBLINS and OUTLAWS
and other scary stuff. There is also
a **HILL** with a **CASTLE** on the top. ↘
In the castle live horrible
Baron Dennis and his
stupid fat wife Prunehilda
who totally **HATE** us
and say that we smell
(which we actually do,
but only a bit)

Also in the castle lives Sergeant
Hengist who shouts at
everyone **ALL** the time
but mostly at ROGER and
NORMAN who are really nice and
friendly and also very useful as they tell
tell us stuff.

You can turn over this page now for stuff about my friends...

# MY FRIENDS who are...

**VERUCCA**

My **VERY** best friend. She's well brave and not scared of anything— except earwigs.

**URK**

Rude words (like BUM) make him giggle and he has loads of **ZITS** and **NITS** that can jump **MILES**.

**EG**

Is scared of pretty much **EVERYTHING** especially hollow trees, the dark, spiders and anything with feathers.

**BURP**

Verucca's litt brother who i **WELL** cool for a small perso

# Chapter One

# TOTALLY THE BEGINNING
# OF THE STORY
# (IT STARTS HERE)

'I reckon people'd pay an awful lot to see tricks like that,' said Robin. Me and my friends were watching Denzel, my pig, do tricks.

'That pig is a totally AWESOME genius,' said Eg. 'We could take him all over the place and charge people to see him and get fantastically rich!'

'There was a man once,' said Urk, 'I think he was my mum's cousin or something. He did that with a chicken. He taught it to dance and catch things and it was well brilliant. He took it all over the place.'

'Wow,' said Eg. 'Did he get very rich?'

'Don't think so,' said Urk. 'I think he got hungry and ate it or something.'

'What do you reckon we could charge people to see Denzel?' said Robin.

I thought it was time I said something. After all, Denzel was MY pig and it was Verucca and me who had spent hours and HOURS teaching him to jump over sticks and fetch things and dance round and round in circles chasing his tail, so I said, 'Hang on a minute. What's all this WE stuff?'

'You're totally right, Sedric mate,' said Robin. 'You and Verucca can get Denzel doing his jumping and stuff and me, Eg and Urk can collect the money. What do you think of that?'

I said that sounded fine, but then I heard my mum screaming, which was most probably because she'd found a rat. My mum's totally terrified of rats, and she goes completely BONKERS if she finds one in our hovel, and because our village is full of rats she screams pretty much all the time. Verucca shouted, 'Hang on

Sedric's mum!' and she went inside to get rid of it.

Then, after Verucca had thrown the rat out (she's TOTALLY brilliant with rats), and my mum had calmed down, there was a lot of shouting coming from the Old Oak Tree, so we went to have a look.

← My mum going completely BONKERS

RAT →

## Chapter Two

# A WEIRDLY FRIENDLY VISIT FROM THE BARON

If there was any shouting in our village, if it wasn't my mum, it was usually Sergeant Hengist. Sergeant Hengist is the sergeant in charge of the castle. He doesn't have ANY manners and he shouts pretty much ALL the time. He also has weird eyes. One's totally normal, but the other one goes all twitchy and rolls around when he's angry, which it does a lot because he's a very ANGRY man. It's confusing because I always want to look at

weird twitchy rolly eye

One good eye

the twitchy, rolly eye, although I mostly try not to look at the sergeant at all because he's really not very nice. Anyway, it WAS Sergeant Hengist, and he was shouting loudly and sticking out his great big chainmail chest.

'PEASANTS OF LITTLE SOGGY-IN-THE-MUD! HIS LORDSHIP THE BARON IS HERE TO PAY YOU ALL A - ER - NEIGHBOURLY VISIT!'

Which was a bit weird. The last time we'd seen the

To the DUNGEONS

US about to be eaten by rats

baron was when he stole my pet pig Denzel and tried to have us taken off to the castle dungeons to be eaten alive by rats.

Baron Dennis lived in the castle with his horrible fat wife, Prunehilda. He took over from his uncle, Baron Osric the Incredibly Old, who died after he had been the baron for at least a HUNDRED years. And even though we were SERFS (which meant that Baron Osric owned us and our

Who sadly **DIED**

R.I.P
OSRIC
THE INCREDIBLY OLD

turnips and the whole entire village) he was really nice and never took our turnips – unlike DENNIS, who took EVERY SINGLE ONE to pay for loads of expensive Roman statues and furniture and a Great

Fat greedy PRUNEHILDA

Big Bubbly Bath Thingy that his greedy wife Prunehilda wanted for the castle. We would definitely have starved to death (because turnips is pretty much ALL we eat), if we hadn't found Osric's will ★.

8

Starving peasant

Departing TURNIPS

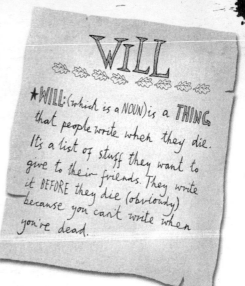

**WILL**

★ **WILL:** (which is a NOUN) is a **THING** that people write when they die. It's a list of stuff they want to give to their friends. They write it BEFORE they die (obviously) because you can't write when you're dead.

In it Osric said

that we were all really

nice and lovely and hard—working and

everything and that he didn't want us to be serfs any

more and that Little Soggy—in—the—Mud was ours to

keep. Forever.

But Dennis tried to get rid of the will and not tell

us what was in it, even though that was TOTALLY

against the law. When we found out what he'd done he

had to give us all our turnips back and he went into

a massive sulk and he hasn't been down to the village

since.

So when Sergeant Hengist said that the baron was

arriving, we were **VERY** surprised, and we were even **MORE** surprised when he appeared the next minute, waving and smiling, even when his chariot got stuck in the mud.

Dennis in **MASSIVE** sulk

'HELLO THERE! LOVELY TO SEE YOU ALL. HOW HAVE YOU ALL BEEN KEEPING?'

**'WHO'S THAT?'** shouted Eg's grandad, who is as deaf as a stick.

**'IT'S THE BARON!'** shouted Eg's mum.
**'HE SAID IT'S LOVELY TO SEE US!'**
**'HAS HE GONE RAVING MAD?'**
shouted Eg's grandad.

'Ssshhh, Grandad,' hissed Eg. 'He'll hear you!'

Two soldiers squelched round to the back of the chariot where they unrolled a long carpet and stretched it all the way across the mud.

'JUST DROPPED BY TO SEE HOW THINGS WERE GOING DOWN HERE IN YOUR LOVELY VILLAGE!' Dennis shouted, stepping down from the chariot on to the carpet.

There were the usual random mutterings from the other grown-ups. 'Well, that's jolly nice of him I must say,' and, 'Kind of him to bring us a carpet,' and other rubbish like that.

'What's wrong with him?' whispered Verucca. 'We all know he totally hates us. Do you think he's gone bonkers?'

'WELL IT'S CERTAINLY LOOKING LOVELY DOWN HERE,' shouted the baron, waving his arms around vaguely at our muddy hovels, and smiling a tight smile. 'I BET YOU ALL LOVE IT HERE IN LITTLE SOGGY-IN-THE-MUD, DON'T YOU, AND YOU'D NEVER WANT TO LEAVE?'

'We're certainly very happy here, your highness,' said Verucca's mum, Mildred, curtseying.

'SOOO PLEASED TO HEAR IT!' shouted Dennis, who was close enough now to stop shouting but for some strange reason didn't.

'He must have gone insane,' said Urk. 'That's it. He's gone

insane, and they had him locked up but he's escaped!'

'Would you like a lovely cup of turnip tea, your worship?' said Urk's mum. 'It's so good of you to come all the way down here to see how we are.'

What is it with grown-ups? Just because Dennis is suddenly being all smarmy and sick-makingly friendly, their memories seem to fail and they've forgotten what a slimy TOAD he really is!

'That's incredibly kind of you but no thank you. I'm just trying to be a good neighbour!' said the baron, his strange tight smile looking even stranger as he got closer. 'So you're all very happy then? Not thinking of moving away at all?'

'Er, no,' said Mildred. 'Whatever gave you that idea?'

The baron didn't answer. He kept smiling but whispered something to Sergeant Hengist, which is when we noticed that the carpet he was standing on was

14

sinking into the mud.

   I moved nearer to hear what he was saying, but I couldn't catch much except, '. . . they're obviously all completely mad but they LIKE it here,' and, 'put our PLAN into action,' and, 'for goodness sake, Hengist, GET ME OUT OF THIS MUD!'

Baron Dennis's FEET →                    ↙ MUD

   Plan? What on earth was he talking about?
   What plan?

## Chapter Three

# MUD AND AN AWFUL LOT OF RUDENESS

As Sergeant Hengist was trying to rescue the baron and his carpet from the mud, Roger and Norman, who were two soldiers from the castle and who were **REALLY** nice, came squelching through the mud towards us.

Roger was carrying a hammer and some nails and Norman had a rolled-up parchment under his arm.

'COME ON! LEFT, RIGHT, LEFT, RIGHT! PICK THOSE FEET UP, YOU POINTLESS PAIR OF FATHEADS, AND GET THAT POSTER UP PRONTO!' shouted the sergeant, who had left some other soldiers to pull the baron out of the mud and on to a dry bit of carpet.

'Sorry, sarge,' said Roger, 'we're going as fast as we can, but what with all the mud and everything I lost one of my boots.'

Norman gave us a cheery wave.

We gave him a cheery wave back just as Roger's other boot got stuck and came right off, and he slipped and dropped his hammer in the mud.

'Oops! Sorry, sarge,' he said.

'GOOD GRIEF! A USELESS TURNIP-EATING TOOTHLESS MUD-CAKED PUSTULAR PEASANT WITH NO BRAIN COULD DO BETTER THAN YOU!' Sergeant Hengist shouted, glaring at us all with his one good eye.

'I think he means us,' said Urk.

'Rude!' said Verucca.

RUDE!

'Right, sarge. I've got it now, sarge,' said Norman, pulling the hammer out of the mud. 'It's a bit messy, Rog. Shall I give it a wipe?'

'Cheers, thanks Norm,' said Roger.

'Just get the blasted poster up!' growled the sergeant, turning round to face us all again.

'PEASANTS OF LITTLE SOGGY-IN-THE-MUD,' he shouted. 'I HAVE A VERY SERIOUS ANNOUNCEMENT TO MAKE!'

Norman unrolled the poster and held it up against the Old Oak Tree while Roger held out a nail.

'You hold the nail, Rog, and I'll hit it with the hammer,' said Norman.

So he did.

'OOWW!' shouted Roger as Norman missed the nail and hit Roger's thumb with the hammer.

'Sorry, Rog – you all right?' said Norman.

18

'It's throbbing a bit but thanks for asking, Norm,' said Roger.

'Give it a suck. I always find that helps,' said Norman.

So Roger sucked his thumb while the sergeant started to turn purple and his weird eye rolled and twitched.

'Would you like to have a little lie-down or a nice cup of turnip tea to help you recover?' said the sergeant.

'Oh, sarge, that's ever so kind of you,' said Roger, 'but I'll be all right in a mo.'

'I DIDN'T MEAN IT, I WAS BEING SARCASTIC!' yelled the sergeant, spraying bits of spit all over the place as he shouted.

'Sorry, sarge,' said Roger, wiping his eye. 'Silly me. We'll just bang these nails in then.'

'Yes. You do that,' growled the sergeant, turning round to face us, his good eye fixing us with a steady stare.

'I HAVE COME HERE TODAY,' he announced, 'TO WARN YOU THAT THERE IS A DANGEROUS CRIMINAL AT LARGE!'

## Chapter Four

# CRIMINALS AND DIRE WARNINGS

The grown-ups gasped and muttered all kinds of random stuff like, 'Ooh, a dangerous criminal. There's a thing. We haven't had one of them before, have we?' and, 'that's nice of the sergeant isn't it, coming all that way down from the castle to tell us?'

Honestly. I ask you.

'A DANGEROUS ANIMAL?' shouted Eg's grandad. 'WHAT SORT OF DANGEROUS ANIMAL?'

Dangerous criminal

Dangerous animal

**'NO, HE SAID CRIMINAL, GRANDAD, NOT ANIMAL!'** shouted Eg.

'THIS MAN . . .' shouted the sergeant, pointing his finger dramatically at the poster that Roger and Norman had finally nailed on to the Old Oak Tree, '. . . IS A RUTHLESS AND DESPERATE AXE-WIELDING OUTLAW WHO HAS RECENTLY ESCAPED FROM THE CASTLE DUNGEONS AND IS NOW ON THE LOOSE. DO NOT APPROACH HIM! HE IS EXTREMELY DANGEROUS!'

Roger and Norman stood back to admire their work. On the poster was a picture of a wild beardy–looking man and underneath it said:

Everyone crowded round to look at the dangerous criminal.

'You want to lock ALL your doors at night and be extremely VIGILANT, well, those of you who have doors to lock,' growled the sergeant threateningly, 'or else he'll be breaking in to chop your heads off while you're asleep!'

There were frightened gasps and more mutterings from the grown-ups.

'WHAT TOTALLY UNEXPECTED AND WORRYING NEWS, SERGEANT!' shouted Dennis from his chariot. 'WELL, MUST BE OFF BACK TO THE CASTLE! IT'S BEEN LOVELY TO SEE YOU ALL AGAIN AND I WILL OF COURSE BE THINKING OF YOU AND THE TERRIBLE DANGER YOU ARE ALL FACING!'

And he waved to us all as the chariot was bumped and dragged through the mud towards the bottom of the hill that led up to the castle.

'Blimey,' said Urk. 'I wasn't expecting THAT.'

'A dangerous outlaw on the loose! Awesome!' said Robin.

Eg whimpered a bit.

'What was that weird expression that the baron had on his face when he said he would be thinking of us?' said Verucca.

'I think he was trying to look concerned,' I said.

'Oh. Was that it?' said Verucca. 'I thought he was constipated or something.'

After the baron and the sergeant had gone, everyone crowded round, trying to have a good look at the picture on the poster.

'That is DEFINITELY a criminal's face, that

is,' said Urk darkly. 'Even if it didn't SAY he was a

dangerous criminal, you'd know

just by looking at him. His eyes

are well close together – that's

always a sign.'

Well mean
and sly
and head-choppy

Eyes
(close together)

'Since when have you become an expert on what

dangerous criminals look like?' said Robin. 'I bet

you've never even SEEN one, and if you had you

most probably wouldn't have known it was a dangerous

criminal. Dangerous criminals don't go around with big

signs saying, "I am a dangerous criminal and I'm going to

chop your head off", do they?'

'My eyes are close together,' said Verucca. 'Does

that mean I'M a dangerous criminal?'

'Well, all I'm saying is he's got a criminal's face. He looks well mean and sly,' said Urk, 'and head-choppy.'

I had to admit that he had a point. Vlad the Bad DID look mean and sly.

'What sort of things has he done then, this Vlad the Bad?' I asked Roger, who was still looking for his boot in the mud.

'Well,' he said slowly. 'He's definitely done some dangerous criminal things and I think he's stolen some stuff.'

I was hoping for a bit more information than THAT.

'How many people's heads has he chopped off, then?' I went on.

'Dunno,' said Norman. 'Don't know much about him really. The sergeant says he's just sort of generally – bad.'

So Roger and Norman actually didn't know any more about this Vlad the Bad than we did, which was interesting.

## Chapter Five

# · SCHOOL

After we said goodbye to Roger and Norman, we headed off to school. There was a lot of arguing on the way about whether dangerous criminals actually **LOOKED** like dangerous criminals or just like everyone else.

I couldn't help wondering why the baron acted like he was surprised when the sergeant announced the stuff about Vlad the Bad escaping from the dungeons. I mean, he would have known already, wouldn't he?

We'd almost reached school when Verucca's little brother, Burp, turned up.

'Sedric,' he whispered. 'Do you want to see my new pet?'

I said I'd love
to. He opened the
top of his pocket
for me to see.

Denzel and I
peered in.

'It's a frog,'
he whispered. 'I've
called it Rabbit.'

'Why have you
called it Rabbit if it's a frog?' I asked.

'Well, I really wanted a rabbit
but I couldn't catch one because
they run too fast,' he said.

RABBIT
(going VERY fast.

I said that was nice
and that I needed to go
into school now. He said
he wished he was big enough to go to school, but I told

him it was WELL boring and he wasn't missing anything, and he went off happily with Rabbit the frog in his pocket.

Gaius, our teacher, was waiting for us outside.

Gaius is a real Roman and he's incredibly old and wrinkly. He stayed here in the village when all the other Romans went back home to Rome, because he doesn't like hot weather and he's allergic to garlic. But to stop himself getting bored on account of there being totally NOTHING to do in our village AND because he's so MASSIVELY clever, he decided to open a school to try to teach us all stuff. He can speak Latin and he reads proper books and he knows about pretty much everything in the WHOLE world, but he also falls asleep randomly in the middle of lessons, which is a Good Thing because then we all get to go outside for extra play.

'Good morning, everyone,' he said. 'I trust there is

a very good reason why you are ALL late?'

'There's a dangerous criminal on the loose, sir,' said Urk.

'Is there?' said Gaius.

'There's a picture of him up on the Old Oak Tree and he looks WELL mean and Sergeant Hengist says he's going to chop our heads off when we're in bed,' said Robin.

'Why would Sergeant Hengist chop your heads off?' said Gaius.

'Not Sergeant Hengist, sir. The dangerous criminal,' said Robin. Urk sniggered.

'He escaped from the castle dungeons and we all have to be VERY careful,' said Eg dramatically.

'Oh dear,' said Gaius. 'That does sound quite alarming. Do tell me more.'

So we told him all about Dennis coming down from the castle in his chariot to ask us if we were all happy living in the village, which he thought was weird too, and the poster of Vlad the Bad and Sergeant Hengist telling us about how he'd escaped from the dungeons and how dangerous he was and everything, and while Gaius was listening to us, Denzel managed to slip past him and into the school.

'Do you reckon he could just be a misunderstood freedom fighter, who accidentally chopped somebody's head off while fighting injustice and freeing the downtrodden poor from poverty?' said Robin.

I said I didn't understand what he was talking about. Vlad the Bad didn't look very misunderstood to me, he just looked mean and scary. Robin said that's how it generally is with freedom fighters, which is why they're misunderstood, then Gaius said that was enough talk about dangerous criminals and misunderstood freedom fighters and could we all please sit down so that he could take the register.

'Urk?' said Gaius.

'Here, sir.'

'Robin? Hood down, please. You know the rules – no hoodies in class.'

'But I need my hood, sir. I'm sitting next to Urk. His nits can jump MILES.'

'Then move away. Sedric?'

'Here, sir,' I said.

'Verucca?'

'Here, sir.'

'Rubella?'

And just at that moment the door burst open and Rubella stood in the doorway, huffing and flicking her hair, with her friend Gert just behind.

## Chapter Six

# PIGS, FROGS AND POINTLESS WALLS

'Sorry I'm late, sir,' she said, and she strolled across the classroom and flopped down on the bench next to me. Gert followed her, waddling silently and picking her zits.

Gains having a doze

'It's just that my mum was having a totally MASSIVE fit about this dangerous criminal wot's escaped,' said Rubella. 'She's well terrified, but I told her no weird escaped criminal was going to mess with me!'

'I don't doubt it, Rubella dear, but I would like to finish the register so I can begin the lesson,' said Gaius.

But before he could, Rubella caught sight of Denzel, who was hiding under the bench.

'OH MY DAYS! That is SOOO gross! Tell him, sir! Pigs an' that should be in pigsties and not be allowed into SCHOOLS! It's disgusting!' she shouted.

'YOU'RE disgusting,' said Verucca,

'and at least Denzel doesn't MOAN all the time.'

'That's because he's a PIG, Verucca Stupidface. Pigs can't talk.'

'Neither can Gert,' said Verucca, 'and she's not a pig.'

Which actually made no sense but I didn't say anything. Urk sniggered, so I gave him a kick. I feel a bit sorry for Gert sometimes.

'And even if Denzel COULD talk,' continued Verucca, 'he definitely wouldn't moan on and on about stuff ALL the time like you do!'

Urk's nits

'I **SO** don't moan,' said Rubella. 'How **DARE** you, Verucca Stupidface, with your stupid curly hair and your big feet!'

'You **SO DO**, Rubella!' shouted Verucca. 'You're always moaning on about how **RUBBISH** it is in our village and how you're going to go off and be **RICH** and **FAMOUS** and have **LOADS** of money. You think you're so much better than us, but you're **NOT!**'

'That's quite enough, girls,' said Gaius firmly as Rubella narrowed her eyes at Verucca.

As I took Denzel outside I thought about how I have learnt a few important things about girls in my life, which are:

**1.** Don't ever make a girl scream. It will **SERIOUSLY** damage your ears.

**2.** Don't ever try to frighten one with creepy

crawlies e.g. spiders or earwigs. They will **NOT** think it's funny (see no. 1, above).

3. Never try to break up girls having an argument because it's pointless.

After I'd come back inside, and the girls had finally finished arguing, Gaius made us do Roman history. It was about this emperor bloke called Hadrian who was famous for building a wall or something.

Hadrian building wall →

← Sheep – being kept in or out. Not sure which.

I don't know why he built it because I wasn't really listening. Maybe he had a lot of sheep he wanted to keep in or something he wanted to keep out. I can't remember. I think if I were famous, I'd like it to be for doing something a bit more interesting than building a stupid wall.

## Chapter Seven

# FiRE AND RAIN

When Verucca and I got back to my hovel at the end of the day, my Mum was having a lie-down, owing to the fact that she was feeling tired and emotional since she heard the news about the escaped dangerous criminal outlaw, **AND** she'd found a rat in the turnips so she'd done quite a lot of screaming.

Mum's always going on about how she wants to move to somewhere where there aren't any rats. My dad says he reckons that there's rats pretty much EVERYWHERE in the world, but as he's never been anywhere but Little Soggy-in-the-Mud, I'm not sure his opinion really counts.

When it got dark, my mum got WELL scared and made my dad barricade the door in case Vlad the Bad came to chop our heads off in the night. She made him push the table up against the door and pile all our chairs on top of the table and put all the pots and pans on top of them, so if Vlad the Bad did try to break in to do horrible stuff to us, it would all fall off and the noise would wake us up.

I thought that if I was going to have my head chopped off, I'd rather NOT be woken up, thank you very much. I'd rather be asleep so I wouldn't know anything about it.

But when I was lying in bed, with Denzel curled up happily on my feet keeping them nice and warm, I heard a weird crackling noise outside, and then I smelt a burning smell and suddenly somebody from outside shouted,

## 'HELP! HELP! THE SCHOOL'S ON FIRE!'

By the time we'd got all the chairs and pots and pans down off the table and opened the door, there were flames leaping up over the school roof. Poor Gaius was there, looking worried, his anxious face all lit up red by the flames. The rest of the village ran around

in the smoky darkness panicking and bumping into each other, while Verucca and I ran to find some buckets to fill with water from the river.

As we ran back to throw the water on to the flames, loads of terrified rats suddenly started falling out of the school roof, where they'd been living, and running around all over the place! This started my mum screaming and going bonkers AGAIN, and she

started bashing at the school roof with her broom, making even BIGGER holes than the fire. So, what with the grown-ups all shouting, 'HELP!' and, 'WE'RE ALL GOING TO DIE!', rats running everywhere and my mum bashing at things with her broom like a lunatic, the whole school would have burnt down if it hadn't started to pour with rain.

Poor Gaius was quite upset.

'I don't understand how it could have happened,' he said. 'It's all extremely mysterious.'

Which was exactly what I was thinking.

It couldn't have been an accident. Things didn't just catch fire in our village. Fires usually went OUT in our village owing to the fact that everything was always so incredibly WET and SOGGY.

It was all VERY strange. But it definitely WASN'T an accident.

## Chapter Eight

# ANOTHER VISIT FROM SERGEANT HENGIST
## (WHICH WAS GETTING A BIT WEIRD NOW)

The next morning, the rain had stopped and the rats had all disappeared. My mum was lying on her bed groaning and going on about how her legs were all wobbly with the shock and she couldn't get up if her life depended on it.

I bet that she COULD have got up if a load of bears came into the village or there was a rat in her bed, but I didn't say so. Anyway – she just carried on and on about how we were all going to have our heads chopped off by Vlad the Bad, or burned to a crisp, or eaten by rats, while Verucca's mum, Mildred, tried to calm her down with lots of turnip tea.

Turnip tea

Verucca and I decided we couldn't really help much so we went outside and found Robin, Eg and Urk waiting for us.

'Why d'you reckon Vlad the Bad set fire to the school?' said Robin.

'We don't actually know it was him,' I said. 'I mean he didn't leave a note or anything saying, "It was me, love Vlad," did he?'

IT WOZ ME
LOVE VLAD
x

'Course it was him and it's because he's bonkers,' said Urk. 'And evil. My dad says bonkers evil people like him don't do things for a reason like you or I might. He does it because he's mean. You can tell just by looking at him.'

'But what was the point?' said Robin. 'He didn't actually HURT any of us, and he didn't STEAL anything so why did he bother?'

'P'raps he just likes setting fire to stuff,' said Urk. 'Like for FUN or something. Some people do.'

Urk actually set fire to the turnip store once. It was totally an accident though. He'd heard that you could start fires by rubbing sticks together, and for ages he just went around rubbing sticks till he got really hot hands, then one day the sticks actually caught fire and he panicked and dropped them. He stopped rubbing sticks together after that because he got in a MASSIVE amount of trouble.

URK rubbing sticks

'I don't think Vlad the Bad would do things just for FUN,' said Verucca. 'He looks much too mean and grumpy to have FUN.'

'Talking of mean and grumpy,' said Eg, 'that looks like Sergeant Hengist over there.'

It was. He was talking to some of the grown-ups, who were listening to him with their mouths open like fish. We went over to have a listen.

'Oh it's definitely the work of Vlad the Bad, all right,' he was saying. 'He's known for doing this sort of thing. Loves stealing things AND setting fire to stuff. He'll probably do some head-chopping next time.'

There were horrified shrieks from the grown-ups.

'HAS HE CAUGHT THIS DANGEROUS ANIMAL YET THEN?' shouted Eg's grandad.

'NO, GRANDAD,' shouted Eg.

'WELL, WHAT'S HE DOING HERE THEN? SHOULDN'T HE BE OUT LOOKING FOR THIS DANGEROUS ANIMAL INSTEAD OF MUMBLING AND BORING US ALL TO DEATH?'

'IT'S NOT A DANGEROUS ANIMAL, GRANDAD! I'VE TOLD YOU BEFORE –

GROWNUPS
*Looking like fish*
←

# IT'S A DANGEROUS CRIMINAL!' shouted
Eg.

## 'WHAT?' shouted Eg's grandad.
## 'A DANGEROUS CRIMINAL? WELL, WHY DIDN'T HE SAY? WHY'S HE BANGING ON ABOUT ANIMALS ALL THE TIME? TELL HIM TO MAKE HIS MIND UP!'

Sergeant Hengist's wonky eye was twitching and rolling around as he tried to ignore Eg's grandad, which was hard on account of all the shouting. Then he narrowed his good eye, lowered his voice and moved closer to us.

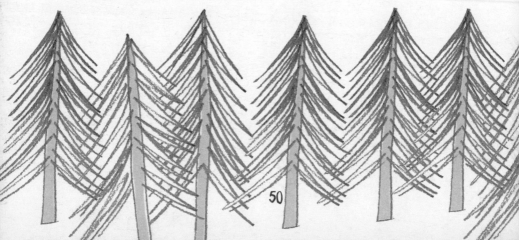

'We have reason to believe that Vlad the Bad is hiding in the Dark Forest and is in league with the dark forces that live there, like trolls and giant hobgoblins and suchlike.' His voice dropped to a gravelly whisper. 'The Forest is a dark and dangerous place . . .'

'Oooh! We know! It's 'orrible in there!' interrupted Robin's mum.

'. . . which is why Vlad the Bad is proving to be so elusive,' growled the sergeant, glaring at Robin's mum.

'What's that mean?' said Urk's mum.

Dark Forest
TROLL
↓

'WHAT?' shouted Eg's grandad.
'LOOSE LIDS – OR WHAT HE SAID!'
shouted Urk's mum.

'It means he's been a bit hard to catch, and that's why they haven't caught him yet,' said Verucca.

How does she know what these words mean? I go to the same school as her and I don't have a clue what 'elusive' means.

'My advice is to move away from here as quickly as possible,' went on the sergeant darkly, 'before he does something much MUCH worse.'

Move troll

## Chapter Nine

# BOGGY-BOTTOM-ON-THE-WOLD

BOGGY BOTTOM ON THE WOLD
(It's WELL boring)

'Right! That's it!' said Robin's mum, after the sergeant had gone. 'We're not staying here a moment longer to have our heads chopped off – or WORSE. We'll move to my sister's in Boggy-Bottom-on-the-Wold. She's got a lovely big hovel. We can stay with her.'

I wondered what could be worse than having your head chopped off.

Robin said he wasn't going to live in stupid Boggy-Bottom-on-the-Wold, because it was

WELL boring and nothing EVER happened there and that he was staying put, so not to bother packing HIS stuff.

Then all the other grown-ups started going on about how they were going to move away to stay with their relations too! I just hoped my mum didn't decide that we should go and live with her grumpy mum and my weird old uncle Bile. That would be bad. My gran moans about totally EVERYTHING and Uncle Bile keeps ferrets and they REALLY stink!

Uncle Bile's
stinky ferrets →

'I'm not going ANYWHERE,' said Verucca. 'No stupid dangerous criminal outlaw is going to drive me away from MY village.'

'I am SO going to move,' said Rubella. 'ANYWHERE would be totally one hundred percent better than living in this boring pile of mud where NOTHING ever EVER happens, and Gert's coming too, aren't you, Gert?'

Gert didn't say anything. She just picked at a big zit.

'Go on then,' said Verucca sniggering. 'No one's stopping you.'

'You think it's funny, Verucca Stupidface. Just you wait. You won't be laughing when I'm living in a castle, with shedloads of gold and servants and posh clothes and jewellery and a proper bed and everything,' said Rubella.

'Come on, girls,' said Robin. 'We have to stick

together and not give in. That's the trouble with the grown-ups. They just give in too easily.'

'I don't think there's anything wrong with giving in easily,' said Eg. 'It's most probably better than having your head chopped off. I quite like the idea of moving away to somewhere there's no dangerous criminal plotting to do horrible things to us or setting fire to us all the time.'

'I think we should talk to Gaius,' I said.

Gaius was wandering about with a bucket of mud and trying to help my dad mend the holes in the school roof, although he seemed to be getting more mud on his toga than on the roof.

'I'm not awfully good at this sort of thing I'm afraid,' he said, 'but I thought I ought to lend your father a hand, Sedric. He's been so kind.'

'I can manage fine on my own thanks, Gaius,' said my dad. 'Anyway, it WAS my Ethel did most of the damage with her broom.'

'Well – if you're sure?' said Gaius.

'Totally,' said my dad. He looked very relieved when Gaius put down the bucket and came to join us. I suppose that even if you have a really enormous brain and read books and talk Latin, it doesn't necessarily mean you're good at EVERYTHING.

'Sir, all the grown-ups want to leave the village. They think Vlad the Bad set fire to the school and that he's going to come back and chop all our heads off,' I said.

'Well – that's what Sergeant Hengist told them would happen,' said Verucca. 'Everyone's terrified.'

'Sergeant Hengist has been down to the village again, has he?' said Gaius thoughtfully. 'I wonder why that is?'

'I reckon he fancies my mum,' said Urk. 'He looks at her funny.'

'No one fancies your mum, Urk,' said Robin. 'She looks like a warthog.'

Urk's Mum →

← A warthog

'That's not very polite, Robin,' said Gaius.

'But it is true, sir,' said Urk. 'She does.'

'Well, whatever your mother looks like, I don't think that Sergeant Hengist is coming down to the village

Clump of trees

because he fancies her,' said

Gaius. 'There must be another reason.'

'What do you mean, sir?' said Robin.

'I'm not entirely sure,' said Gaius thoughtfully,

'but I think we need to find out, and due to the

temporary absence of a school hovel, how do you all

fancy a nature ramble?'

'What sort of a nature ramble, sir?' I said.

'One that could possibly take you all up the hill

towards the CASTLE,' said Gaius, 'to see what you

might find. I, of course, will need to stay here to clean

up the mess, but I am SURE you are all more

than up to the task,' he added, winking.

To the
CASTLE

'The CASTLE?' said Rubella looking interested.
'YOU aren't coming,' said Verucca.
'I SO am,' said Rubella.

## Chapter Ten

# A BIT OF NOT VERY
# SUCCESSFUL SPYING
## (IN WHICH WE DIDN'T FIND OUT VERY MUCH)

So we all set off up the hill towards the castle. Me, Verucca, Urk, Eg, Robin, Rubella, Gert and Denzel.

We started off doing it in Stealth Mode, but what with Rubella complaining about everything REALLY loudly and Urk tripping over tussocks★ all the time and Denzel tripping us up we decided to just walk normally.

### TUSSOCK

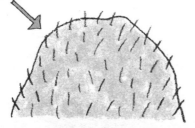

★ Tussocks: Random mounds of earth with grass growing on them. Not much use except for tripping over or for very small animals to hide behind.

We'd gone about half way up the hill when we heard voices coming towards us, so we hid behind a bush. It was a quite a small bush so it was a bit of a squash, and we were only just in time as Dennis and a very posh-looking man in a toga suddenly appeared from the direction of the castle.

'You'd be a fool to miss this chance, Boris, old man. It simply can't fail!' Dennis was saying as they walked down the hill towards us.

'Are you calling me a fool, Dennis?' said the other man.

'No, no of course not!' said Dennis

quickly, going pink, 'I'm just saying that it's a DEAD CERT in the money-making department. Ah, Hengist! There you are!' he said as the sergeant suddenly appeared from out of nowhere.

'Could I have a word, sire?' said the sergeant.

'Of course, Hengist. Boris, do take the plans,' said Dennis. 'You will have a good view of the village just through those trees over there. I'll be with you in a minute.'

Boris strode over to a clump of trees on the edge of the hill, while Dennis looked around nervously and lowered his voice.

'So, Hengist. How did it go?' he whispered.

I tried to hear what was being said but Dennis was talking too quietly, so I shuffled forward through the bush to get a bit nearer.

Eg kept wriggling about behind me.

'Keep still!' whispered Verucca.

'I can't,' he hissed, 'I'm sitting in an ants' nest!'

'Well, move!' hissed Verucca.

'Can't! OW! I've been stung,' Eg hissed back.

What with everyone making a noise behind me, I missed most of what Dennis had to say, but I caught a bit at the end.

'. . . and she KEEPS ordering all this expensive

stuff from Rome. I told her I can't afford it. You can't M♽VE for statues and sofas, and there are mosaics on every wall, and now she's bought these ridiculous chairs! Frankly, Hengist, I'm at my wits' end! I really need this plan to work or I may have to sell the castle!'

'Don't worry, sire,' whispered the sergeant. 'My next plan will DEFINITELY do the trick. I am going to . . .'

'Eg, get your elbow out of my ear!' said Robin.

'Ssshhh! I can't hear!' I hissed at everyone.

'I can't help it. You wouldn't like it if you were sitting in an ants' nest, would you?' complained Eg.

'OW! You're squashing me and there's a load of nettles here! Eg, move your foot!' whispered Urk.

'This is totally boring rubbish,' hissed Rubella. 'We haven't even SEEN the castle. I didn't come all this way to get stuck behind a bush with you lot. Come on,

Gert, we're going home.'

'You can't!' whispered Verucca. 'They'll see you!'

'So?' said Rubella, starting to get up.

'You'll ruin everything,' hissed Robin, sitting on her.
'Just shut up and wait!'

'GET OFF
ME!' shouted
Rubella.

'Ssshh!!'
hissed

Rubella - not happy
↓ (but then she
never is)

Verucca loudly.

'What was that?' said the sergeant. 'I thought I
heard something!'

We all held our breath, but then something stopped
Sergeant Hengist in his tracks.

## Chapter Eleven

# WHICH IS MAINLY ABOUT STUPID POSH PEOPLE BEING POSH AND STUPID

'THESE CHAIRS ARE ABSOLUTELY THE VERY LATEST THING FROM ROME, LUCRETIA!' A voice like a rusty wheel wafted down the hill towards us.

Us holding our breath ← behind bush.

'ARE THEY QUITE SAFE, PRUNEHILDA?' came another voice.

'OH, PERFECTLY! EVERYONE USES THEM IN ROME! THE STREETS ARE JUST FULL OF THEM - YOU SIMPLY CAN'T MOVE WITHOUT BUMPING INTO ONE!' Prunehilda screeched back.

At the sound of her voice, Denzel got **VERY** excited and I had to grab him to stop him running out from behind our bush. Denzel has a **HUGE** crush on the baron's fat wife, Prunehilda. Not sure why.

**'HANG ON TO HIM!'** hissed Verucca, as Denzel tried to wriggle out of my arms. 'Or he'll get us all in **HUGE** trouble again!'

As
I clung
on to
Denzel,
I could see
Prunehilda. She was
sitting on a wooden chair with
long handles that was being carried down
the hill by Roger and Norman. Her voice sounded
all wobbly and she was a funny shade of green, because
Roger and Norman were completely out of step with
each other and the chair was rocking about all over
the place. Behind Prunehilda, on another chair, was a
tall thin woman dressed in a toga with a very sneery
expression on her face like there was a bad smell
under her nose.

'All right your end, Norman?' shouted Roger from
the back.

'My arms are a bit achey but thanks for asking, Rog,' shouted Norman.

'Shut up about your stupid arms,' hissed Prunehilda. 'Just put me down here before I throw up!'

'Righty-ho,' said Norman, dropping the chair on to a tussock. It wobbled a bit and then tipped over. Prunehilda slid off the chair and landed in an undignified heap on the grass. Her fancy hair, which was piled high in a complicated construction of curls, had slipped down the side of her head and was dangling over one ear.

'Sorry, your ladyship!' said Roger. 'The ground's a bit lumpy here! Shall we find you a nice flat bit?'

'Just stop talking and go away before I have you both executed for being STUPID!'

Prunehilda hissed at them. She picked herself up unsteadily and rearranged her hair. 'And if you EVER do that to me again, I'll have you scrubbing out the toilets for a month!'

Then she turned round and smiled a tight smile at the woman in the chair behind. 'IT'S SUCH AN ORIGINAL WAY TO TRAVEL, DON'T YOU THINK, LUCRETIA?' she shouted.

The soldiers carrying the other woman had found a flat bit to put her down on.

'Oh, it's delightful!' said Lucretia, getting down from the chair. 'Although Boris and I go everywhere by chariot these days!'

'Oh DO you?' said Prunehilda through gritted teeth. 'How lovely!'

'MY DARLING PRUNEHILDA AND DEAR LUCRETIA! THERE YOU ARE!

# YOU'RE JUST IN TIME! BORIS IS HAVING A LOOK AT THE PLANS,'

shouted Dennis, emerging from the clump of trees and taking both the women by the arms.

They headed back to the trees and I signalled to the others that I was going to try to get a bit nearer so I could hear what was going on, but I didn't manage to because there was lots more scuffling behind me, and Urk whispered very loudly for Eg to get his foot off his head.

'I'm trying,' whispered Eg, 'but the ants . . .'

'Swap places with me then,' hissed Verucca angrily, and then there was a lot of noise and someone said, 'OW!'

'What's that noise? Someone's spying on us, Dennis!' squawked Prunehilda, coming out from the trees.

'Go and have a look, Hengist,' ordered Dennis.

Eg's nose bleeding →

Nettles

I turned round.
Urk had his face
in the nettles and Eg's
nose was bleeding.

'We have to get out of here, NOW!' I said.
We all crept backwards out of the bush
as fast as we could, and as soon as
we were clear we legged it back
down the hill.

Us legging it down the hill →

## Chapter Twelve

# SOMETHING IN THE DARK

We went straight to Verucca's hovel. Urk finally stopped complaining about the nettle stings after Verucca's mum, Mildred, gave him a big piece of her special turnip and blackberry cake – but his face came up in horrible big red lumps, so Mildred smeared it with some stuff she'd got from Mad Warty Edna, who is a weird old witch who makes **VERY** suspicious potions. It smelt **DISGUSTING**, but Urk said he quite liked

the smell. He even ate some of it.

Eg's nosebleed went on for hours. Eg's nosebleeds are legendary. He once had one that lasted for THREE days. It was EPIC.

Rubella had gone off in a huff, dragging Gert with her, on account of she said we'd tricked her into going because she never even SAW the castle and she told Urk she hoped he would puke after eating the disgusting potion.

I told everyone what I'd heard and we worked out that:

1, Prunehilda was STILL stupid and greedy and totally bonkers about anything Roman, e.g. men in togas, stupid naked statues, Great Big Bubbly Baths, people speaking Latin, being carried everywhere on a chair, etc.

2. Prunehilda's expensive taste was causing Dennis sleepless nights and he was worried he might have to sell the castle.

3. The baron and Sergeant Hengist were **DEFINITELY** up to something dodgy and I might have found out what it was if Urk hadn't fallen in the stinging nettles.

Plotting something DODGY

We needed to find out more.

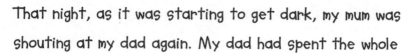

That night, as it was starting to get dark, my mum was shouting at my dad again. My dad had spent the whole

day trying to load up all our furniture on to the turnip cart so we could leave the village but then he had to take half of it off again to barricade ourselves in.

He'd put the table up against the door again and was piling more stools and pots and pans on top.

'Hang on, Wilfred,' said my mum. 'P'raps you shouldn't put that table there. What if Vlad the Bad sets fire to the whole village this time? We'll be trapped in here! Do you want us to be burnt alive in our beds?'

So my dad took all the chairs and pots and pans

back down again, but then my mum said, 'But what if

we HAVEN'T got anything up against the door and

then he breaks in and chops off our heads while we're

asleep?'

'For goodness sake, Ethel!' he shouted. 'Either I

DON'T put the table against the door

and we all get our heads chopped off, or I

DO put the table against the door and we

all get burnt to a frazzle!'

So my mum said, 'I think we need a

bigger table, Wilfred. That table isn't

nearly big enough. Sedric! Go and see if

you can borrow a bigger table!'

'But it's dark out, Ethel,' said my dad.

So Denzel and I slipped outside quickly,

before they had the chance to argue about

THAT as well.

It was lovely and peaceful outside in

the darkness. A big half moon lit up the village, and I could hear scratching noises as rats scurried about in the shadows.

I knew I wouldn't be able to find a bigger table, but I figured if I stayed out long enough, my mum might have calmed down, so I sort of wandered about. Then I saw a Verucca-shaped figure coming towards me in the darkness. She was muttering to herself.

'Why on earth are grown-ups so STUPID? Why can't they think about things a bit more instead of just going totally BONKERS and deciding to LEAVE the village?'

'Don't ask me,' I said. 'My parents are driving me INSANE. They can't decide whether or not to put stuff up against the door.'

'What?' said Verucca.

'It's all about whether we'd rather burn to a crisp or have our heads chopped off by Vlad the Bad,' I said.

79

'Don't worry about . . .'

Suddenly Verucca put her hand over my mouth.

'Ssh!' she whispered. 'Did you hear that noise?'

'What noise?' I said.

'That noise!' said Verucca, pulling me into the shadows. 'There's someone coming!'

Then I heard it. A horrible rasping voice in the distance.

'BEWARE, PEASANTS OF LITTLE SOGGY·IN· THE·MUD,' it growled from the darkness.

Suddenly, from out of the gloom, a huge

lumbering figure came lurching towards us. It was
big and shaggy with hair like straw, and it wore
a ragged cloak that trailed through the mud. It banged
loudly on all the hovel doors with a big stick as it
passed.

Doors opened
and people
looked out,
screamed and
slammed them shut
again.

'THIS IS
A WARNING!
BAD STUFF IS
GOING TO
HAPPEN!'
it growled.

'DO NOT IGNORE THIS WARNING! YOU MUST ALL LEAVE IMMEDIATELY OR VLAD THE BAD WILL GET YOU ALL!' and then it banged on a few more doors and disappeared into the shadows again.

'Whatever was THAT?' said Verucca, as Denzel suddenly raced off into the darkness after the weird shaggy figure.

'WOAH! DENZEL!' I shouted, 'COME BACK!'

But he ignored me and kept on running, until he caught the bottom of the thing's raggedy cloak in his teeth. Underneath the cloak I caught a glimpse of something shiny, like chainmail, glinting in the moonlight, just before it disappeared into the darkness.

## Chapter Thirteen

# TROLLS, MOLES AND HOBGOBLINS

The next morning, everyone in the village had gone even **MORE** bonkers, and they were all arguing about what the thing had been the night before.

Urk thought it was a werewolf and his mum thought it was one of her cousins who'd gone a bit strange a while back, but the general opinion was that it was a troll.

Urk's mum's cousin
(gone a bit strange)
↓

'It were a giant troll come to **KILL US ALL!**' cried Mildred.

'No, it weren't!' said Eg's mum. 'I reckon it were a hobgoblin!'

'It were **DEFINITELY** a giant troll,' said my dad.

'Most probably sent from the Dark Forest by Vlad the Bad to scare us to death, like the sergeant said.'

'What's all this, then?' said Sergeant Hengist, who had suddenly appeared from nowhere, puffing out his chest as usual and looking pleased with himself.

'Somebody talking about me?'

'He might as well move into the village,' I said to Verucca. 'Seeing as he's here so often.'

Verucca sniggered and Sergeant Hengist glared at us with his one good eye.

'**OOH! YOU WERE SO RIGHT, SERGEANT!**' shouted Mildred. 'We had a visit last night from something **'ORRIBLE!**'

'Oh dear,' said the sergeant. 'Oh dear, oh dear, oh dear. Vlad the Bad's definitely plotting something **FIENDISH** – no doubt about it. Sending one of his **TROLLS** down to warn you. It's what he does, you see.'

'Did anyone actually **SAY** it was a troll?' I said, but no one was listening.

'Well, it's certainly scared me,' said Eg's mum. 'I'm not staying here a moment longer. I'm not going to wait until I get eaten or terrified to death or **WORSE!**'

The sergeant wandered away, tutting and sucking his teeth and going on about how DANGEROUS it all was and, as he did, I noticed he had some straw sticking out from under his helmet and some smudges of mud on the back of his neck.

'WHAT'S ALL THIS ABOUT A GIANT MOLE?' shouted Eg's grandad.

'NO, GRANDAD,' shouted Eg. 'It was a giant TROLL, not a mole!'

Giant MOLE

'WELL, THAT MAKES MORE SENSE,' shouted Eg's grandad. 'I NEVER HEARD OF A GIANT MOLE. I HOPE IT DIDN'T TOUCH MY CONKER COLLECTION. THEY'RE DEVILS FOR CONKERS, TROLLS ARE.'

Troll playing with conkers

'I think you're all being a bit hasty,' I said. 'What if it was just someone dressed up trying to scare us?'

'Well they're doing a good job, is all I can say,' said my dad. 'Your mum hasn't stopped screaming since last night!'

It was true. We could hear her.

'Sedric's right,' said Verucca. 'What if it's just someone trying to frighten us into leaving the village? If we go now we'll never know, will we?'

'And if we don't go, who knows what Vlad the Bad will do to us!' said Eg's dad.

'Shouldn't we all stay and fight?' said Robin. 'After all, we OWN this village. It's ours. Osric gave it to us. We can't just give it up!'

But no one was listening. The grown-ups were all too busy packing up their things to take any notice of us.

And I suddenly realised that the grown-ups

actually believed all the stuff about the trolls and the hobgoblins and the dragons and things that they said lived in the Dark Forest, which was quite a scary thought. I always thought they'd made it up to stop us going in there. But it wasn't as scary as the thought that we might all actually have to leave Little Soggy-in-the-Mud.

## Chapter Fourteen

# DREAMS AND POTIONS

There was nothing left to do. No one was listening to us, so Verucca and I went inside to see how my mum was.

'All right, Sedric's mum?' said Verucca.

'Oh, don't ask, Verucca love,' my mum said. 'I won't get up because I can't. I've completely lost the use of my legs. They've gone all wobbly on account of that thing

My mum (nerves in shreds)

Wobbly legs

last night, and that dangerous criminal outlaw Vlad the Bad still out there on the loose waiting to do horrible things to us. My nerves are in shreds and I haven't shut my eyes all night and I doubt if I'll ever sleep again.'

'Never mind,' said Verucca. 'I had a REALLY weird dream last night. Do you want to hear it?'

I was going to say that now probably wasn't a VERY good time. Verucca's dreams are VERY long and rambling but she started anyway.

'Well, it began with us all lost in the Dark Forest – except it wasn't actually the Dark Forest because all the trees were pink and could talk and frogs were jumping about all over the place, and then there was a huge Roman

Flying chariot

91

chariot thing that flew over us like
a bird, and Denzel – I think it was
Denzel but it was sort of half–pig
half–rabbit – fell down a massive hole
. . .' but then I stopped her because
my mum had gone a funny colour and
she started screaming about us all
being doomed so I pushed Verucca
outside. I didn't think her dream was
really helping my mum's nerves, plus
they could totally go on for HOURS.

Denzel / Rabbit falling down hole

My dad was pacing up and down outside like a not–
very–happy ferret in a small cage, and Verucca's mum,
Mildred, was trying to calm him down.

'I'm at my wits' end, Mildred,' said my dad. 'She just
won't stop screaming and carrying on. I've made her
some turnip tea and told her we'll move to her mother's
but she just won't listen! I wish I had a magic potion

or something to calm her down.'

I was just thinking that Wits End sounded like an actual place, like where people could go when they went a

bit weird, when Verucca whispered, 'What about Mad Warty Edna? She makes potions for all sorts of things. I bet she's got something for stopping people from screaming!'

'AND she's also totally bonkers and lives in a pile of sticks in the Dark Forest,' I said. 'I wouldn't go anywhere near the Dark Forest, not if you gave me a great big massive bag of

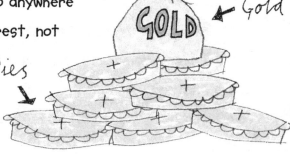

← Gold

Pies ↘

gold **AND** a lifetime's supply of turnip pies.'

'She doesn't actually live **IN** the Dark Forest, she lives on the edge, and she's only a tiny bit bonkers,' said Verucca, 'and if we can get your mum to calm down she may not want to go and live with your moany old gran and your smelly uncle Bile, and we **DEFINITELY** need some time to try and find out what's going on.'

I had to agree. I wasn't happy about it, but there was nothing else for us to do as none of the grown-ups would listen to reason, so we went to find Robin, Urk and Eg. Robin and Urk said they'd definitely come because the grown-ups were driving them mad too. Eg didn't want to come because he said that Mad Warty Edna was well scary and weird and she kept toads and things and he was terrified of toads, and he didn't want to go anywhere near the Dark Forest because it was full of trees with holes in and things with feathers as well as all the other scary stuff like trolls and

dragons and giant hobgoblins and they terrified him too.
But he didn't want to stay in the
village either, what with his
grandad shouting about
moles and dangerous
animals all the time
and worrying about his
conker collection, not

Eg's grandad's →
conker collection

to mention his mum packing all their stuff.

And then, when Eg was STILL trying to decide
what to do, Mildred arrived with Verucca's little
brother, Burp. She said we had to look after him
because she was worried that if she took her eyes
off him, what with all the packing she had to do, he'd
wander off and Vlad the Bad would get him. We said

he would be perfectly safe with us, which wasn't a TOTAL lie. We just forgot to say that we were going to the Dark Forest. Verucca said it was best we didn't mention it to her mum, as she'd only worry.

Rubella and Gert arrived and Rubella said, 'What would Mildred worry about?' so Verucca told her to mind her own business, and Rubella said that she'd tell Mildred unless we told her where we were going.

So we told her.

In the end, we took some turnips in case we got hungry, and me and Denzel, Burp and Verucca, Eg, Urk, Robin, Rubella and Gert all set off along the path to Mad Warty Edna's cave. Eg had finally decided that he would come with us, but he really wasn't happy about it.

We'd been walking for a little while when suddenly Gert said, 'This Mad Warty Edna, is that her real name then?'

We all stared at her with our mouths open. Gert

97

never usually said **ANYTHING**.

'I s'pose that's her real name,' I said. 'The 'Mad' bit is because she's as mad as a box of weasels.'

'And she's called 'Warty' because she's got warts everywhere,' said Urk.

'Oh,' said Gert, picking at her zits. 'I won't be buyin' any of her wart potions then.'

As we got closer to the Dark Forest it started to get a bit scary. I looked into the very dark darkness and tried to ignore the rustling and snuffling noises and Eg whimpering about how terrifying it all was and how he'd really like to go home now. It was a relief when we finally reached a cave on the edge of a thicket of trees.

A sign outside said:

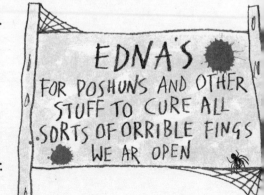

EDNA'S
FOR POSHUNS AND OTHER
STUFF TO CURE ALL
SORTS OF ORRIBLE FINGS
WE AR OPEN

We looked around but we couldn't see anyone.

'P'raps she's off collecting stuff,' said Eg.

'What, like roots that give you the squits, you mean?' said Robin, sniggering.

'It wasn't my fault,' said Urk. 'She told me they were OK and I only did it once.'

'Yeah, and like the mushrooms she put in a potion for my mum,' said Robin. 'My mum had this really bad toothache, and Mad Warty Edna made her this potion and it made her go all giggly and daft and she started seeing elves and fairies

everywhere. It didn't wear off for days – it was WELL funny!'

'Maybe we should all go and look for her,' said Verucca. 'She can't be far. The sign says "open".'

'It always says that,' said Urk, 'even when it's not. It most prob'ly says it in the middle of the night, although I s'pose as she's a witch she might be open then. Witches do WELL weird stuff in the night.'

Then we heard a croaky voice.

'If it's potions yer after, you'll have to come back later,' it said. 'I'm havin' me breakfast.'

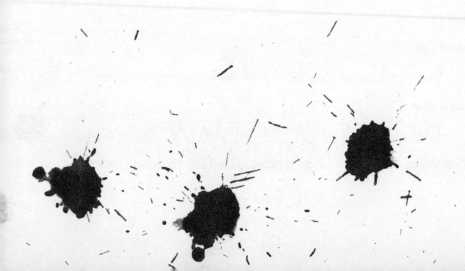

## Chapter Fifteen

# FROGS, WORMS AND A LOT OF VERY WEIRD STUFF

The voice came from underneath a pile of sticks.

'But the sign says "open",' I said.

'You don't want to believe everyfing you reads. Take my advice. Some people is GREAT BIG LIARS!' said the voice.

'Ask her when we CAN come back,' whispered Verucca.

'You ask her,' I whispered back.

'No,' said Verucca. 'It's your mum that won't stop screaming!'

'WON'T STOP SCREAMIN'?' said the voice, as the pile of sticks started to move. 'Why didn't you say so 'stead of standing there like turnips talkin' gibberish? I got lots of lovely potions for people what won't stop screamin'!'

First two fat toads plopped out from under the pile of sticks, and then out wriggled Mad Warty Edna.

She stood up, wiping her mouth and belching.

Toads plopping ou

'Worms,' she said. 'I loves to start the day with a couple of nice fat juicy worms.'

Eg whimpered and Rubella gagged and said she was TOTALLY going to throw up.

'So – is that a potion for people what's screamin' a BIT or screamin' a LOT that yer wantin'? Because I've got one here can shut a person's mouth fer ages! D'you want that one?'

'No, thank you,' I said. 'It's for my mum. She's just a bit worried about stuff.'

'Right. Follow me then, and DON'T TOUCH ANYTHING!' she said as she led us into her cave.

'I'm not goin' in THERE!' said Rubella. 'It's WELL stinkin' and rank. Come on, Gert. We're stayin' outside.'

She was right, actually. It smelt REALLY bad and there was weird horrible stuff EVERYWHERE. There were dead things hanging from the roof, and

bottles and
jars full of
tiny legs and eyes and
things. The bad smell was coming
from a steamy cauldron that was bubbling over
a fire. As I got closer I accidentally breathed some in
and went a bit dizzy so I stepped backwards, tripped
over Denzel and fell into a massive sticky spider's
web.

'Verucca,' whispered Burp. 'I don't like it in
here!'

He pointed upwards to where a couple of
wrinkled dried-up frogs were dangling from the
cave roof.

'Oh dear,' said Verucca. 'I see what you mean.

Why don't you play outside? We won't be long.'

Burp looked much happier and skipped outside, his hand in his pocket holding on to Rabbit the frog.

Edna peered shortsightedly at the dusty bottles on the ledges as she ran her bony finger over the names. 'Right. We got potions for taming wild dragons, spoilt princesses, 'orrible trolls, and this one 'ere's a powerful love potion,' she said, turning to us and

105

grinning a hideous toothless grin. 'This one's for curin'
toothache – no, it's not. I think that one's rat poison.
Potion for bad breath, not sure what that one is,
potion to make your hair fall out, potion to stop your
hair falling out – ah. Here we are – potion for calmin'
down folks worried about stuff. That's the one you're
after,' she said as she lifted the bottle down. 'Tis
strong stuff, mind. Tell 'er only take a tiddling sip else
she'll lose the feeling in 'er legs – or was that the
potion for dizziness?'

I was beginning to wonder if she knew
what any of her potions actually did
when she said to Urk, 'Pass me them
bones in that there bowl, child.'

He passed her the bowl
and she stuck in her bony
hand. She grabbed a handful
of small white bones and

threw them to the ground, then she squinted at them for a while, muttering to herself, and she stood

Bowl of bones

back and said, 'There'll be scrittlin' munties afore sundown and the bats'll be flying northeast again. Let this be a warnin' to ye and remember to boggle yer nettles afore ye go.'

'Why is she talking like that?' whispered Eg.

'I don't know,' I whispered back. 'I don't have a clue what she's on about.'

'How did you DO that?' said Urk. 'How could you tell all that stuff you just said, just from throwing some bones?'

'It's magic, that's what it is, young sir,' she said, spitting on the bones before scooping them up and putting them back in the bowl, and then she wiped the potion bottle on her filthy cloak and handed it to me.

'You got somethin' to pay me with?' she said.

I looked at the others. I'd completely forgotten about paying.

'Give her some turnips,' whispered Verucca.

So I gave her two.

'S'pose they'll do,' Edna said grudgingly, 'if you ain't got nuffin' else. But I don't eat 'em. They're disgustin',' she said, putting them in her pocket. 'They'll come in 'andy fer throwin' at people I don't like. If yer 'ungry, you can't beat a nice fat juicy worm in my opinion.'

It was nice to get out into

← Rubella looking BORED

the fresh air again and out of the strange sickly
mixture of smells.

Rubella was leaning against a tree inspecting her
nails and looking bored.

'Where's Burp?' said Verucca.

'How should I know?' said
Rubella.

'He came outside when he
saw the dead frogs,' I said.
'You must have seen him.'

'Oh yeah! Snotty kid
with the frog!' said Rubella.

'So where is he?' I
said.

'He went off,' said
Rubella.

'WHERE?' shouted
Verucca.

*Verucca getting REALLY angry*

109

'Um. That way I think,' said Rubella waving her hand vaguely. 'It was after he tripped over my foot. Stupid kid should've looked where he was going.'

'YOU TRIPPED HIM UP? WHAT IS WRONG WITH YOU?!' shouted Verucca.

'Don't get your thingummies in a tangle,' said Rubella. 'It was an accident. That horrible frog fell out of his pocket and he chased off after it. I don't know where he went. He's not MY snotty little brother, he's yours. You should have been looking after him, shouldn't you, Verucca Stupidface!'

'Just shut your mouth, Rubella!' shouted Verucca, but I could see that she knew Rubella was right. She was supposed to be looking after Burp.

'Well, I'm not hanging round here any more,' said Rubella. 'You coming, Gert?'

'BUT WHERE DID BURP GO?' shouted Verucca.

Gert, who had been waddling off
after Rubella, suddenly stopped and turned
round.

Then she pointed into the Dark Forest.

Gert pointing into the
DARK FOREST →

## Chapter Sixteen

# IN THE DARK FOREST AND IT'S NOT VERY NICE

The trees closed round us as we walked into the Dark Forest and I shivered. It suddenly felt very cold.

There was no sign of Burp anywhere.

'What if he's been eaten or Vlad the Bad's taken him?' whispered Verucca.

'He'll be fine,' I said as cheerily as I could, although I didn't really believe myself. 'He's not been gone long.'

'We have to find him, Sedric! Whatever will I say to my mum if we don't?' said Verucca, setting off wildly through the undergrowth.

I said I didn't know, but then I said maybe we should

all shout out his name really loudly so he'd know where we were.

So we did. We all shouted as loudly as we could, but then we heard howling in the distance and some horrible growling noises in the undergrowth close by.

'I think we should stop shouting,' whispered Verucca.

Black feathery thing
caw-cawing off

Suddenly something big and black and feathery flapped out of the undergrowth in front of us and went caw—cawing off over the treetops.

'**AAARRGGHH!**' screamed Eg, grabbing my arm. '**WHAT WAS THAT?**'

'It was just a bird,' I said, trying to sound calmer than I felt. 'Relax.'

'**RELAX?**' shouted Eg. '**ARE YOU MAD?**'

'Ssshh!' hissed Verucca. 'Something will hear you!'

'I think the whole forest heard you!' said Robin. 'If you **WANT** to be

eaten that's fine by me, but will you PLEASE shout somewhere else?'

So Eg kept quiet, except for squeaking and jumping at every tiny sound. Then Urk whispered, 'I don't want to worry anyone or anything, but I think we're being followed.'

We all stopped and turned around very slowly.

'I think it's me,' whispered Robin. 'I'm behind you.'

'Oh, right,' said Urk. Then he pushed a branch out of the way and let it go, smacking Robin in the face with it.

'We're never going to find Burp like this, are we?' whispered Verucca. 'He could be anywhere.'

'P'raps if we all split up and went in different directions, we'd have more chance of finding him,' suggested Robin.

'WHAT?' shrieked Eg, flapping his arms. 'Are you INSANE? What if we meet a huge troll or a giant hobgoblin or a load of wild bloodthirsty outlaws or something?'

Random head-chopping OUTLAW who's a bit cross →

'BURP'S OUT THERE SOMEWHERE!' shouted Verucca, 'AND HE'S SMALL AND ALL ALONE!'

'I WAS JUST SAYING!' Eg shouted hysterically. 'WHAT I MEAN IS, AT LEAST WHEN THERE'S FIVE OF US ALL TOGETHER, THE TROLLS AND HOBGOBLINS AND THINGS CAN'T EAT US ALL AT ONCE, AND WE'D BE A TINY BIT SAFER IF WE MET SOME RANDOM OUTLAWS WITH HEAD-CHOPPING AXES WHO MIGHT DECIDE TO KILL US ALL AND STEAL STUFF FROM US — EXCEPT WE HAVEN'T GOT ANYTHING TO STEAL SO THEY'LL PROBABLY JUST KILL US ANYWAY BECAUSE WE'VE MADE THEM CROSS!'

'WE NEED TO ALL STOP SHOUTING!'

I shouted. 'WHAT ABOUT THE TROLLS AND THE HOBGOBLINS AND EVERYTHING HEARING US?'

That quietened everyone down, but I had to admit Eg had a point. We did need to stick together.

So we carried on, going deeper into the Dark Forest, whispering Burp's name as loudly as we dared.

Then it started to rain. It splattered on the treetops and dripped down our necks, and the deeper we went, the closer together the trees got, and the undergrowth got more scratchy and tangly.

'Did you know that the Romans actually eat DORMICE?' I said, trying to take our minds off how miserable and scared we were, 'and those big fancy birds with long tails — what are they called?'

'Peasants?' said Urk.

'Peacocks,' said Verucca. 'We're peasants. I think you mean pheasants.'

'I saw something move,' whispered Eg. 'It was definitely a giant hobgoblin, or a werewolf. Over there! Look!'

He pointed. A squirrel ran up a tree.

'Have you ever actually SEEN a giant hobgoblin or a troll or even an outlaw, Eg?' asked Robin. 'Proper live ones, I mean – not just ones from your overactive imagination.'

'I can't help it if I'm sensitive,' said Eg miserably. 'I'm not like you. You're not scared of anything. My mum says I've got an anxious nature.'

Squirrel

'Why don't you try some of Mad Warty Edna's potion, then?' said Verucca. 'She said it was for calming folks down who are worried about stuff – and that's definitely you. You're worried about pretty much EVERYTHING.'

Eg looked a bit nervous. 'I'm not sure,' he said.

*Mad Warty Edna's potion*

'Just try a little sip to see if it works,' said Verucca, handing him the bottle. Eg took a massive swig and choked.

'Hey! Hold on! I said just a bit!' said Verucca.

Eg's eyes went a bit weird for a second.

'Well?' I asked.

'Don't know,' he said. 'I'm feeling a little bit sort of

– floaty – but it's hard to tell . . . Yeah, actually I do feel a bit more relax–'

But he didn't finish what he was saying because just then another huge and feathery thing croaked loudly and flew out of a hole in a tree just in front of him. Eg screamed and ran off through the trees. We watched him go quite a long way, then there was another sort of scream and he was suddenly gone.

Eg had totally vanished.

'Blimey,' said Urk. 'That was weird.'

## Chapter Seventeen

# IN WHICH A LOT OF DISAPPEARING GOES ON

We stood in the Dark Forest looking through the trees at where we had last seen Eg.

We were cold, wet, lost and  scared. The only one who was cheerful was Denzel. He loved the rain and was running round in happy circles chasing his tail.

I thought how nice it must be to be a pig, and not worry about anything except where the next meal was coming from.

Denzel chasing tail

He didn't know that we were in danger of losing our homes and that Eg had disappeared and that little Burp was lost somewhere out there in the dark and dangerous forest.

I decided that when I died I'd quite like to come back as a pig.

'Do you reckon it was the potion?' said Urk. 'P'raps Mad Warty Edna gave us a disappearing potion by mistake.'

'There's no such thing as a disappearing potion,' I said.

'How do you know?' said Urk. 'If people that took the disappearing potion just disappeared you wouldn't know, would you? You'd just think they'd gone somewhere else.'

'What are we going to do now?' said Robin.

'We could all go home,' said Urk.

'How could you even THINK that?' said Verucca furiously. 'What if it was you out there lost and frightened? How would you feel if we all just gave up and went home because it got a little bit SCARY?'

'I was just saying,' he said. 'There's no need to get all grumpy.'

'So we carry on searching for Burp and Eg, then? Agreed?' said Verucca.

'Agreed,' we all said.

'Let's go then,' said Robin, setting off in front.

So we all followed Robin along the muddy path we had last seen Eg running down, but we hadn't gone very far when we heard a scream and a noise like falling rocks and then Robin disappeared from view.

'ROBIN'S DISAPPEARED TOO!' shouted Verucca. 'THERE'S SOMETHING SERIOUSLY WEIRD GOING ON! WILL EVERYONE PLEASE STOP DISAPPEARING?'

125

'NOW can we go home?' Urk said. 'There's some really bad stuff going on here. That troll thing said, "BAD THINGS WILL HAPPEN". This must be what he was talking about!'

'Of course it's not!' I said. 'There has to be a sensible explanation for all this. We just have to find out what it is.'

'Well I don't want to stay around just in case

there 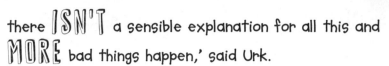 a sensible explanation for all this and
**MORE** bad things happen,' said Urk.

'Well, **GO** then, said Verucca angrily. 'We'll be just
FINE without you!'

Urk looked a bit uneasy.

'What? On my own? Actually I think I'll hang around
a bit more with you . . . Hey! Look at that!' he said.

Denzel doing
somersault

'Denzel did a somersault!' and as he stepped back to

watch Denzel, there was a sound of falling rocks and Urk suddenly disappeared down a big hole that was hidden between some massive tree roots.

'OOWW!' came a voice from the hole.

'I'VE FOUND EG AND ROBIN!' shouted Urk.

We peered into the hole and down into the darkness and saw three pale faces looking up at us.

Massive HOLE

Robin↓  Eg↓  Urk↓

Well, two were just pale and the other was pale but with blood all over it.

'ARE YOU HURT?' shouted Verucca.

'I WASN'T UNTIL URK LANDED ON ME!' shouted Robin. 'BUT EG'S GONE A BIT WEIRD.'

'I haven't god weird,' said Eg. 'I've just got a bassive dosebleed, but I'b feeling buch better dow. I feel quite relaxed actually. You haven't got ady bore of that potion, have you, Sedric?'

I threw the bottle down to him.

'JUST A LITTLE SIP, NOW!' I shouted down. 'REMEMBER WHAT MAD WARTY EDNA SAID – AND I NEED SOME LEFT FOR MY MUM! VERUCCA AND ME ARE JUST GOING TO FIND SOMETHING TO PULL YOU OUT – LIKE A LONG BRANCH OR SOMETHING!'

'RIGHTY-HO!' shouted Robin. 'WE'LL SEE IF THERE'S A WAY OUT DOWN HERE!'

Verucca and I went off to search for a long branch to rescue Urk, Eg and Robin, while Denzel snuffled about in the undergrowth.

130

Suddenly he stood quite still, sniffing the air and looking around. He sniffed some more — and then he went running off through the trees.

'DENZEL!' I shouted. 'STOP! WHERE ARE YOU GOING?'

'Come on, Sedric!' shouted Verucca, pulling on my arm. 'We need to follow him! He might have found Burp!'

'What about the others?' I said. 'We can't just leave them!'

'They'll be fine down there,' she said. 'Come on!

Denzel running off

But Denzel was already a long way off.

'Stupid pig! I just hope you know where you're
going!' I said as Verucca and I ran after him, slipping
and sliding in the mud and tripping over tree roots,
until he stopped – right on the edge of a rocky cliff.

Denzel ran round in excited

circles, wagging his little

tail, but just as I had

nearly reached

him, he

slipped

on

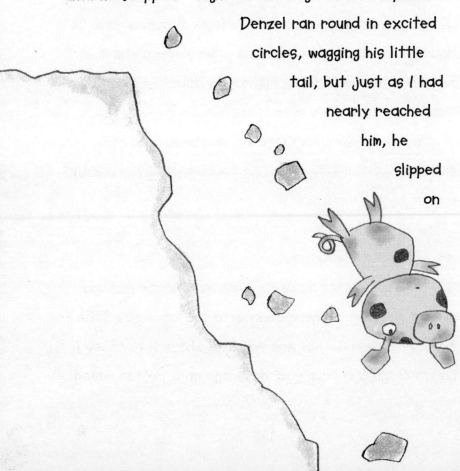

the edge and fell, tumbling and sliding down to a clearing at the bottom.

'DENZEL! ARE YOU OK?' I shouted, and a strange growly voice came up from below. It said, '. . . and then the happy little bunny went hoppity hop all the way back to his burrow where his mummy and daddy and all his little bunny brothers and sisters were and . . . Hey! What's that pig doing here?'

'DENZEL!' shouted a small voice.

'BURP!' shouted Verucca excitedly, and she slithered all the way down the rocky cliff and landed in a heap next to Denzel.

So I followed them. It seemed like the only thing to do, but it did hurt rather a lot.

The clearing we landed in was outside a cave and sitting on a log in the entrance to the cave was little Burp. And next to him was someone whose hairy face I had seen just a couple of days ago on a poster nailed to the Old Oak Tree.

It was Vlad the Bad.

## Chapter Eighteen

# VLAD THE BAD?

## 'YOU GET AWAY FROM MY BROTHER!'

shouted Verucca, pulling Burp off the log and clutching
him tightly.

Vlad the Bad was very surprised, and looked like
he was about to say something when Robin, Eg and Urk

came bursting out from the back of the cave.

'HEY YOU GUYS! WE TOTALLY FOUND A WAY OUT!' shouted Urk, 'THERE WAS THIS SORT OF TUNNEL THING AND . . . !'

He stopped as they all saw who was sitting on the log.

'LOOK! IT'S HIM OFF THE POSTER!' yelled Robin. 'IT'S VLAD THE BAD! LET'S GET HIM!'

Him off the poster jumped up. He looked at Verucca and me, and then back at Robin, Eg and Urk, who were covered in mud and blood and **DID** look quite alarming, and he ran off towards the trees.

'AFTER HIM!' shouted Robin.

'YEAH, DUDE! LETS TOTALLY GET HIM!' shouted Eg, chasing after him.

Dude? When had Eg started saying stuff like 'dude'?

'Could someone tell me why we're chasing Vlad the Bad?' panted Urk. 'The well-known dangerous head-chopping criminal?'

'Because if we catch him we won't have to leave the village!' I shouted.

'How do you work THAT out?' said Urk.

'Just do it!' shouted Verucca, taking Burp by the hand and thundering after Eg and Robin.

'But he's not . . .' squeaked Burp, but we couldn't hear anything else over the noise of Eg's bloodcurdling yells and us pounding through the muddy undergrowth.

Robin, Eg and Denzel had almost caught up with him. **'GET HIM, ROBIN!'** shouted Eg, **'GO FOR HIS LEGS!'**

**'WHO ARE YOU?'** shouted Vlad the Bad, **'AND WHY ARE YOU CHASING ME?'**

'He's pretending he doesn't know,' panted Urk.

'But he **DOESN'T!'** shouted Burp.

'What do you mean?' I said.

**'HE'S NOT A BAD MAN! HE'S REALLY KIND! HE FOUND RABBIT AND HE'S BEEN TELLING ME STORIES AND EVERYTHING!'** shouted Burp.

**'WAIT!'** I shouted, but I was too late. Eg rushed at Vlad the Bad, swinging a massive branch, yelling, **'AARRGGHH!'** like a total wild man and walloping

Vlad around the head.

Vlad tripped over Denzel and then fell to the ground like a tree.

## Chapter Nineteen

# SOME WRONG THINGS FINALLY EXPLAINED

Vlad the Bad didn't look as scary when he was knocked out. He looked quite nice. He smelt **WELL** bad though. Burp was furious.

'Why didn't you listen? I've been trying to tell you that he's not bad, and now it's too late because you've **KILLED** him!' he shouted, glaring at Eg.

But Eg wasn't listening.

There was a mad gleam in his

Eg with mad gleam in eye →

eye as he ran off towards the trees, waving his big stick and shouting, 'RIGHT! WHO'S NEXT?'

'Why's Eg gone all weird?' asked Burp.

Then Vlad the Bad groaned.

'Where am I?' he said. 'My head REALLY hurts.'

'YOU'RE NOT DEAD!' shouted Burp, doing a happy dance and giving Vlad a big hug.

'We're really sorry about Eg hitting you,' I said, 'he's not usually like that. It was Mad Warty Edna's potion, you see, it made him all relaxed and stuff and THEN we all thought you were Vlad the Bad, the dangerous head–chopping criminal outlaw . . .'

'What?' Vlad said. 'Hold on there! What you goin' on about? I'm not a dangerous head–chopping whatever–you–said outlaw. I've never chopped no one's head off.'

'But aren't you Vlad the Bad?' said Verucca.

'No. Well, yeah. But, no. What I mean is, my name IS Vlad,' he said, looking very confused, 'but not Vlad the BAD.'

'I hope someone else gets what he's on about,' said Urk, as we all helped Vlad the most–probably–NOT–Bad–after–all to his feet. 'Because I don't.'

So we told Vlad all about the poster with his picture on it, and what Sergeant Hengist had said about him.

**'BUT HE'S TELLING STONKIN' GREAT BIG LIES! HE TOLD ME HE WAS LETTING ME OUT OF THE DUNGEONS 'COS THEY NEEDED THEM FOR SOMEONE ELSE!'** shouted Vlad.

'Hold it right there,' interrupted Verucca. 'Are you saying that Sergeant Hengist LET you out of the dungeons? You didn't escape?'

'No. Why would I escape?' said Vlad. 'I loved it in there. It was warm and dry and they fed me regular — and there was all me little rat friends, Bernard and Molly and all their little ones. I was SO happy.'

Their little ones

Bernard and Molly

'So why did the sergeant let you out?'

'Don't know,' said Vlad. "im and the baron just come down to visit me a while back and told me I was free to go, and they said it'd been a pleasure 'avin' me. They was very nice. I can't believe they told all them lies about me! I'm REALLY hurt now,' and he sniffed and wiped his nose on his sleeve.

'So why did the sergeant say that you were a dangerous head—chopping criminal if it wasn't true? I don't get it!' said Urk. 'Although you DO actually look a bit like a dangerous criminal, if you don't mind me saying. You've got that sort of face.'

'I gets it from me dad,' said Vlad, "cos he really WAS a criminal. He wanted

**Vlad & Family**
For Head Choppin and
Stealin Fings
Reasonubel Rates

Small Vlad running away

me to join the family business, which was choppin' off heads and thievin' but I didn't want to so I ran away. I did do some thievin' but I were rubbish at it. That's how I got caught and put in the dungeons. I never been no good at nothin'.'

'I'm sure you're good at SOMETHING,' said Verucca kindly. 'Everyone's good at SOMETHING. But now we really have to get back to the village to show everyone that you're not dangerous after all, if they haven't already left!'

The rain had stopped by the time we all began to walk back through the Dark Forest. Eg had calmed down quite a lot, because the potion was wearing off and he'd stopped shouting and behaving like a lunatic.

'That's a nasty bump you've got on your head there. How did you get that?' he said to Vlad.

'You done it,' said Vlad, 'with that great huge stick

of yours.'

'Was that me?' said Eg. 'I'm terribly sorry.'

'Don't you remember?' said Robin. 'You ran out of the cave yelling like a mad person and then you hit Vlad over the head and knocked him out. You were amazing!'

'Was I?' said Eg, looking proud and embarrassed at the same time.

'How's Rabbit?' I asked Burp.

'He's OK,' said Burp, 'but I think I'm going to put him back in the ditch where I found him. Vlad said that frogs aren't really meant to live in people's pockets. He said he'd help me find a proper rabbit of my own.'

## Chapter Twenty

# THE GRAND ROMAN EXPERIENCE THING

We'd walked for quite a while when Robin turned round and said, 'Does anyone actually know where we are? It's just that I think we've passed that tree a couple of times before. I only know because I noticed it's got a bit sticking out that looks like a bum.'

Urk sniggered.

The word bum always makes him snigger.

I said I sort of assumed he knew where he was going which was why we were all following him.

'I was just walking,' said Robin. 'I thought that you'd stop me if I was going the wrong way.'

'We're lost, aren't we?' I said.

'Yes,' said the others.

'What's the pig doin'?' said Vlad.

Denzel was all excited. His ears were pricked up

and he was sniffing.

'He does that,' I said. 'It's probably just acorns.'

'He seems to know where he's goin',' said Vlad as Denzel suddenly raced off through the trees. 'Reckon we should follow 'im?'

So we all ran after Denzel until the trees began to get thinner and it looked like we'd finally reached the edge of the Dark Forest. Then we heard voices coming from the other side of the trees.

There were three very loud posh voices and one that sounded exactly like a rusty wheel. Prunehilda!

Denzel was still running.

'STOP HIM, SEDRIC!' hissed Verucca.

I threw myself on top of him just as Prunehilda's voice rang out.

'It's going to be absolutely HUGE. The chariot racing track will be over there,' she squawked, and I could hear her jewellery jangling as she waved her arms about, 'RIGHT next to the bath house which is going to be simply GORGEOUS, and there'll be all sorts of lovely wine bars and restaurants all dotted about all over the place. Nothing tacky of course,' she said, 'it's all going to be absolutely the very best and FRIGHTFULLY expensive of course!'

'I do believe they're called thermopolia in Rome,' said Lucretia.

'What are?' said Prunehilda.

'Restaurants,' said Lucretia, 'but of course if

you'd BEEN to Rome, like Boris and I have, you'd KNOW.'

'And you're quite sure the disgusting peasants are all actually going to leave?' said Boris. 'I don't want to waste my money investing in this stinking muddy village and then find they're all staying put.'

'Of COURSE they're going,' laughed Dennis. 'Hengist here scared the PANTS off them, didn't you, Hengist? LOOK! Can you see? They're over there packing up all their scabby furniture!'

'The totally slimy lying TOAD!' said Verucca. 'How DARE he?'

'It really will be THE place to visit, Lucretia. Anyone who is ANYONE in high society will be coming here for the complete Roman experience,' squawked Prunehilda.

'I simply can't WAIT!' said Lucretia. 'Although I don't suppose it will be as good as the REAL thing. Boris and I are off to the Mediterranean on a cruise next month, aren't we, Boris?'

'How totally DELIGHTFUL for you both!' said Prunehilda, although she didn't sound like she thought it was delightful at all. She actually sounded like she would quite like to kill Lucretia.

'What ARE they going on about?' said Urk.

'Don't you get it yet?' I said. 'Dennis and Sergeant Hengist have been trying to scare us into leaving the village so that Dennis could build whatever stupid Roman thing it is they're going on about and make loads and loads of money!'

'But they can't DO that!' said Robin. 'This is OUR village!'

'Then we'd better go and tell the grown-ups what's going on, and stop them from leaving before it's too late!' said Verucca.

When we got to the village, everything was packed up and ready to go. Chairs and tables were piled high on the turnip cart, and there were sacks full of turnips

US all getting quite angry

VLAD THE BAD
Extreemly dangerus outlaw
WANTED
For hed chopping and
steeling Kings

Sacks full
↰ TURNIP

Egs grandad looking
for his conkers

156

and more sacks filled with other stuff, all in a big heap
under the Old Oak Tree.

Eg's grandad was wandering about complaining that
his conker collection had been moved AGAIN, while
poor Gaius was trying hard to persuade everyone not
to leave.

Then Vlad caught sight of the Wanted poster with
his face on it.

'Blimey, it's ME!' he said, but at the same time,
Eg's mum saw him too.

'AAARRGGHH! IT'S HIM!! IT'S VLAD
THE BAD COME TO KILL US!!' she
screamed.

Grown-ups all going
BONKERS →
and running about

**'IT'S THAT VLAD THE BAD – THE DANGEROUS HEAD-CHOPPING CRIMINAL OUTLAW!'** shouted everyone.

'It's not **HIM**, mum,' said Verucca. 'Well it **IS** him, but it's **NOT** – and anyway he isn't going to hurt anyone! He's **NOT** a dangerous criminal . . .'

**'OF COURSE HE IS – JUST LOOK AT HIM!'** screamed Mildred. **'YOU HAVE TO LISTEN TO US!'**, shouted. **'HE REALLY ISN'T DANGEROUS – HE'S QUITE NICE, HONESTLY!'**

But no one **WAS** listening, of course. Why did I ever think they would? They were all too busy screaming and being stupid and running about.

158

Mildred grabbed hold of Verucca and Burp and dragged them away, screaming, 'YOU JUST GET AWAY FROM THEM, YOU – YOU – CRIMINAL!'

Then suddenly, in the middle of all the bonkers screaming and fainting, a voice shouted, 'STAY RIGHT WHERE YOU ARE! YOU'RE ALL UNDER ARREST!'

ME trying to make the grown ups listen

# Chapter Twenty-one

# ALMOST THE END

Sergeant Hengist pushed his way through the crowd, puffing out his huge chainmail chest and looking even MORE pleased with himself than usual.

'Oh thank goodness you're here, Sergeant,' said Mildred. 'You're just in time!'

'They've caught that evil Vlad the Bad!' said Eg's mum. 'Did you say we're ALL under arrest, sergeant?' said Gaius. 'You surely don't intend to arrest the children?'

Sergeant Hengist
(very pleased with himself)

160

'I RATHER THINK I DO!' shouted Sergeant Hengist. 'I'M ARRESTING THEM FOR HELPING A DANGEROUS CRIMINAL OUTLAW!'

'But I'm not a dangerous criminal outlaw,' said Vlad. 'You and the baron said so. You said I was a model prisoner when you . . .'

'SHUT UP!' yelled the sergeant, pushing his face up close to Vlad's and growling. 'You can say what you like. No one's going to believe YOU – a head–chopping thieving outlaw – are they? It's your word against mine.'

'WHAT'S GOING ON, HENGIST?' shouted Dennis as his chariot was pulled through the mud where it squelched to a halt.

'I'VE JUST ARRESTED VLAD THE BAD, SIRE!' said the sergeant.

'Have you? Well done!' said Dennis, smiling his weird

tight smile. 'That was very – er quick! I rather thought he would be on the run for a bit – er – longer?'

'OH GOODY! WE'RE JUST IN TIME TO SEE YOU OFF!' squawked

BYEEE!

Prunehilda, as she, Boris and Lucretia were all carried into the village on their stupid Roman chairs. She waved and her bracelets jangled noisily. 'It's SUCH a shame you all have to go, but never mind – I'm sure you'll all be VERY happy in whichever squalid mud-soaked stinking place it is you're going.'

'Well, don't delay them, my sweet,' said Dennis. 'They probably have quite a long way to go.'

'It's not going to be the same here without the
peasants, is it sarge?' sniffed
Roger, dropping Prunehilda's
chair down in the mud.
'Why do you suppose
they're going?'

Roger and Norman
getting a bit teary
⇒

'I have no idea, corporal,' snapped the Sergeant,
'but let's not hold them up.'

'It wasn't anything to do with you, was it, sarge?'
said Norman.

The sergeant's wonky eye started going round and

he went a funny colour.

'I don't know what you mean, corporal,' he said.

'Don't you remember, sarge? That little trick you said was an April Fool's joke to scare the villagers, when you dressed up as that troll thingy. You looked SO funny, didn't he, Rog?'

'Corporal, will you just SHUT UP!' growled the sergeant.

But it was too late. We'd all heard everything and it all made perfect sense.

'You made EVERYTHING up!' I shouted at Dennis. 'You got Sergeant Hengist to start the fire and dress up as the troll and you tried to make us believe that Vlad the Bad was behind it all and that he was REALLY dangerous, but it was all LIES to scare us into leaving OUR village!'

One of Boris's peasants in the **STOCKS** → (Old Dark Ages punishment)

'That smelly little peasant is calling you a liar, Dennis!' said Boris. 'I really don't know why you put up with such rudeness. I'd have MY peasants put in the stocks for that!'

'Things are a bit different here, Boris,' said Dennis wearily, 'thanks to my fool of an uncle.'

'But why did you do it?' I said. 'We weren't hurting you, were we?'

'OF COURSE YOU WERE!' he shouted, the big purple vein in his forehead beginning to throb. 'DID YOU THINK WE WERE HAPPY TO GO ON LIVING

IN OUR LOVELY CASTLE WITH YOUR DISGUSTING VILLAGE RUINING OUR VIEW, DAY AFTER MISERABLE DAY, WHEN WE COULD GET RID OF YOU ALL AND BUILD SOMETHING WONDERFUL THERE INSTEAD? I WAS GOING TO MAKE SO MUCH MONEY . . .' and he sat down on the chariot step with his head in his hands.

'But it hasn't WORKED, has it?' I shouted. 'Because now we know the truth and WE'RE NOT GOING TO LEAVE!'

A huge cheer went up as everyone FINALLY understood.

Prunehilda still didn't, though.

'So, aren't the peasants leaving then, Dennis?' she squawked.

'No, my sweet!' said Dennis, wearily. 'They're NOT.'

BRILLIANT!

'BUT YOU PROMISED ME! YOU TOLD ME YOU HAD IT ALL UNDER CONTROL - YOU SWORE THAT WE WOULD FINALLY BE RID OF THEM!' she shouted as she collapsed back on to her chair in a faint. 'OH, DENNIS, I'M HAVING ONE OF MY TURNS!' she squawked as Roger and Norman carried her away.

'Never mind, dear,' said Dennis weakly. 'I'll get Hengist to run you a nice hot bath.'

Prunehilda having one of her turns.

Chapter Twenty-two

# PRETTY MUCH THE END NOW

Once everything had all been unpacked and put BACK into our hovels again, and life had pretty much got back to normal, we all had a  party. It did take quite a while to convince our parents that Vlad the Bad wasn't really bad at all, even though he did have a proper criminal's face, but in the end they all felt so sorry for him that everyone invited him to come and live in the village with us.

Vlad got VERY emotional. I don't think he'd had very nice life, what with his dad being a dangerous criminal and everything, so he wasn't used to people actually being kind to him. When my dad asked him if he didn't mind sleeping in the pigsty till we'd built him a hovel of his own, he said that he'd really rather live in the pigsty on account of all the rats, as it reminded him of the dungeons and Molly and Bernard and all their little ones, and then he got all teary and emotional all over again, and Gaius had to give him a clean hanky.

After the party, Vlad and Burp took Rabbit the frog to the ditch together and watched as Rabbit plopped back into the muddy water. Burp was sad to see him go but he did agree that he seemed much happier, and Vlad promised he'd show him how to catch a real rabbit all of his own.

Rabbit the Frog plopping into the ditch

And at the end of a **VERY** long day, when everyone had finally gone indoors, I sat with Gaius and Denzel under the Old Oak Tree and watched the sun go down behind the trees.

'We did it, didn't we Gaius?' I said happily. 'We TOTALLY saved the village.'

'You certainly did, young Sedric. If it wasn't for you, Verucca, Eg, Urk and Robin, you would all probably be living in Little Piddle-on-the-Marsh by now, or Boggy-Bottom-on-the . . . where was it?'

'Wold,' I said.

'Ah, yes, and neither of those places could EVER be as nice as Little Soggy-in-the-Mud, could they?' said Gaius.

Me, Denzel and Gaius all happy →

GET YOUR WOBBLE ON AT
# JELLY PIE CENTRAL
.CO.UK

PARP!

WELCOME TO A WORLD OF
## SILLY JOKES, WACKY GAMES & CRAZY VIDEOS!

Jelly & Pie
the game

Bungee pants

Download the AWESOME free apps now
for hours of jelly-tastic gaming.

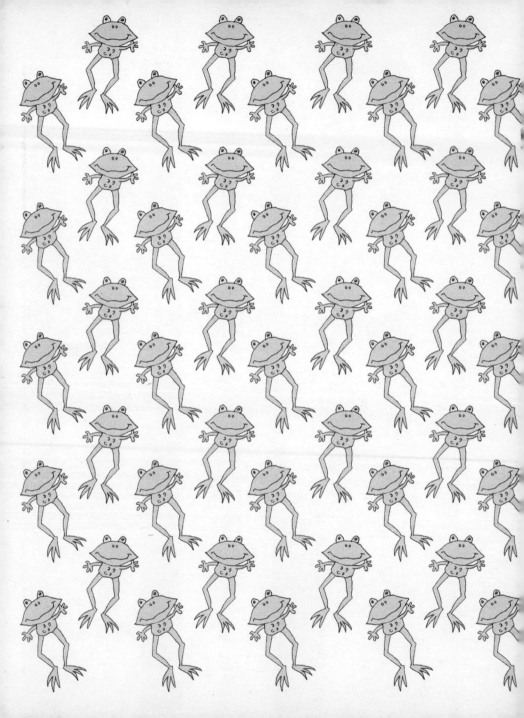